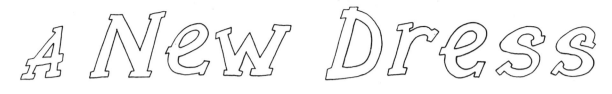

A New Dress for Maya

For Neil with love and affection
and for Wendy

— M. B.

For a free color catalog describing Gareth Stevens' list of high-quality children's books, call 1-800-341-3569 (USA) or 1-800-461-9120 (Canada).

Library of Congress Cataloging-in-Publication Data

Blackman, Malorie
   A new dress for Maya / story by Malorie Blackman ;
illustrated by Rhian Nest James. — North American ed.
      p.   cm.
   Summary: Longing for a new dress from the store, Maya
is disappointed to attend a party in a dress made by her
mother, but she receives a pleasant surprise when she
sees what the other girls are wearing.
   ISBN 0-8368-0713-8
   [1. Clothing and dress—Fiction. 2. Parties—Fiction.]
I. James, Rhian Nest, 1962-   ill. II. Title.
PZ7.B532337Ne   1992
[E]—dc20   91-50337

North American edition first published in 1992 by

Gareth Stevens Children's Books
1555 North RiverCenter Drive, Suite 201
Milwaukee, Wisconsin   53212, USA

First published in Great Britain in 1991 by Simon & Schuster
Young Books. Text copyright © 1991 by Malorie Blackman.
Illustrations copyright © 1991 by Rhian Nest James.

Printed in Mexico

1 2 3 4 5 6 7 8 9 97 96 95 94 93 92

A New Dress for Maya

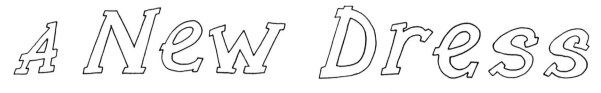

By Malorie Blackman
Illustrated by Rhian Nest James

Gareth Stevens Children's Books
MILWAUKEE

Maya was sad. Maya was mad.

"Grandma, I want a new dress to wear to Anna's party tomorrow," Maya sighed.

Grandma rocked slowly. Back and forth, back and forth. "Your Mamma's making you a dress," Grandma replied.

Maya stomped her foot. "I want that dress in Mr. Muldoon's shop window."

"But the dress your Mamma's making for you will be the prettiest dress at the party," Grandma smiled.

And Grandma rocked. Back and forth, back and forth. But Maya just couldn't smile back.

Maya pouted. Maya shouted.

"Daddy, may I have the dress in Mr. Muldoon's shop? I'd look really good in that dress."

Daddy turned the soil in his garden. Up and over, up and over.

"But you'll look great in the dress your Mamma is making for you," Daddy smiled.

"But I want the one in Mr. Muldoon's shop," Maya pleaded.

Daddy didn't seem to hear her. He just smiled and dug up some more dirt. Up and over, up and over. But Maya just couldn't smile back.

Maya sighed. Maya cried.

"I'd be the happiest girl at the party if only I had the dress in Mr. Muldoon's shop," Maya thought out loud.

Her brother Ben threw his ball against the wall and caught it as it fell. Up and down, up and down.

"Who cares about a silly dress?" Ben said.

"Ben," Maya said, "All my friends will be wearing new dresses to Anna's party."

"Who cares about them?" Ben shrugged, and smiled. And he threw his ball against the wall again. Up and down, up and down. But Maya just couldn't smile back.

Maya breathed deep. And had a good weep.

Dotty the dog was chasing her tail. Around and around, around and around.

"Oh, Dotty," Maya said. "I want that dress in Mr. Muldoon's shop so much."

"Woof!" Dotty barked. And she chased her tail again. Around and around, around and around. But Maya couldn't even smile at her silly dog.

Maya just wandered around, past the neighbors and through the town. She walked to Mr. Muldoon's shop. Outside the window, she stopped.

There was her dress – the dress she wanted so badly. She wanted it more than chocolate drops or soda pops. She wanted it more than a trip to the zoo or a new hairdo. She wanted it more than anything.

"Hello, Maya," said Mr. Muldoon. "Have you come to buy a dress?"

Maya shook her head.

"These dresses are very popular," Mr. Muldoon smiled. "Shall I save you one?"

Maya shrugged. She was too sad to speak. And she just couldn't smile back.

That night, Maya stared dreamily at the moon. "If only I could have that dress in Mr. Muldoon's window . . ."

But the moon, like everybody else, didn't seem to hear her.

The next day, when it was time to go to Anna's party, Mamma smiled. "Here's your new dress, Maya."

Maya was sad and mad and she pouted and shouted and sighed and cried — all at once!

"I don't want that stupid dress!"

"You can wear this dress or not go to Anna's party at all," Mamma said. "You'll have to make up your mind."

So Maya wore the dress.
And she HATED it.

Mamma walked Maya down the street to Anna's house. Maya just looked down at the ground and frowned and frowned.

She didn't even look up when they passed
Mr. Muldoon's shop.

"Here we are at last," Mamma said.

"Hi, Maya! You're just in time," called out Anna's Daddy. "We're playing hide-and-seek in the back yard. Come on. Everybody's hiding! You can help me find them!"

First Maya found Sarah,

then Pumpkin and Peter,

then Fay,

then Vijay and Victor,

and Mara and May.

Then Emma and Eddie and Heather together.

Hey! That was funny. Wow! That was odd.
All the girls at the party were like peas in a pod!
Each wore the dress that she'd wanted to wear.
So hers was the only different dress there.

Maya laughed as they played inside and smiled as each said,

"Your dress is pretty . . ."

"Your dress is best . . ."

"It looks really good . . ."

"I like your new dress!"

"Thank you," said Maya. "My Mamma made it for me."

Soon Anna's Daddy called out, "It's time for some delicious cake!"

Anna blew out the candles on her birthday cake and her Daddy took a picture.

"Say 'Cheese!' Smile please!"

Maya was glad and no longer sad.

As they walked home, Maya skipped beside Mamma. "Thanks for the dress," Maya sighed.

"You're welcome," Mamma winked.

And they both smiled.